YOUTH FICTION

Wish Upon a Star

Iris Howden

Published in association with
The Basic Skills Agency

Hodder & Stoughton

Acknowledgements
Cover: Stephanie Axtell
Illustrations: Maureen Carter

Orders; please contact Bookpoint Ltd, 39 Milton Park, Abingdon, Oxon OX14 4TD. Telephone: (44) 01235 400414, Fax: (44) 01235 400454. Lines are open from 9.00–6.00, Monday to Saturday, with a 24 hour message answering service. Email address: orders@bookpoint.co.uk

British Library Cataloguing in Publication Data
A catalogue record for this title is available from the British Library

ISBN 0 340 77605 6

First published 2000
Impression number 10 9 8 7 6 5 4 3 2 1
Year   2005 2004 2003 2002 2001 2000

Typeset by GreenGate Publishing Services, Tonbridge, Kent.
Printed in Great Britain for Hodder and Stoughton Educational, a division of Hodder Headline Plc, 338 Euston Road, London NW1 3BH, by Atheneum Press, Gateshead, Tyne & Wear

Wish Upon a Star

Contents

1

Jenny

Jenny moved to the front of the stage.
She took a bow.
'More, more,' the audience called out.
They wanted her to sing again.

After the concert the matron of the
old people's home came onto the stage.
'That was lovely, Jenny,' she said.
'Thank you so much for giving up your time.
Let's give a big hand for Jenny Scott.'

Jenny stood there as the clapping went on.
She could see her gran in the front row.
She looked very happy.
Jenny went up to her.
'Come on, Gran,' she said. 'Time for bed.
I'll take you to your room.'

The old lady looked at the photo
on the table next to her bed.
'Your Mum would have been proud of you
tonight, Jenny,' Gran said.
'It was good of you to come and sing for us.'
'I don't mind,' Jenny said. 'I enjoyed it.'

'I'm glad you sang, "Softly Softly",' Gran said.
'I love that song.
Ruby Murray used to sing it.
She was a sweet girl, with a lovely voice,
just like you.
Not like these punks you get nowadays.'
Jenny had to smile.
Gran was always way behind the times.

'Do you want me to close the curtains?'
Jenny asked.
'Yes please, dear,' Gran said.
As Jenny stood at the window she saw
a streak of silver fall across the night sky.
'Look Gran, a falling star,' she said.
'Quick, make a wish,' Gran said,
just as she had when Jenny was a little girl.

Jenny shut her eyes. What to wish for?
She didn't really need anything.

Last year had been a really bad year.
Her mother had died after a long illness.
Now Jenny's life
was starting to take shape again.
She had a job, good friends,
a steady boyfriend.
What more did she need?

Yet there was something missing.
Part of her wanted more from life.
Being on stage tonight had felt good.
Singing always made her feel like that.
Even here, singing old time songs
to a few old people.
When she sang, she was in another world.
It was as if she really came alive.

'Is your young man picking you up?'
Gran asked.
'Ian? No. He's busy tonight.'
Jenny didn't tell her gran
that they'd had a row.

It was the golf club dance that night.
She'd told Ian she couldn't go.
He'd been angry.
'You're missing the dance to sing
to a bunch of old folk,' he'd said.
'Well thanks a lot!'

'I'm sorry, Ian,' Jenny told him.
'It was fixed up ages ago.
Gran and her friends are looking forward
to the concert. I can't let them down.'

Sometimes it was hard to stand up to Ian.
He was her boss at the supermarket
as well as her boyfriend.

Gran didn't really like Ian.
She thought he was too old for Jenny.
'You're only just 18,' Gran had said.
'Don't tie yourself down too soon.
There's a big wide world out there.
Plenty of time before you settle down.'

Jenny thought about her words as she ran
down the drive.
She wished Ian was coming to meet her
in his smart new car.
Instead, Dad sat waiting in his old banger.
Poor Dad. He'd gone to pieces after Mum died.
Things got even worse when he lost his job.
He seemed to give up all hope.

It had been up to Jenny to help him.
She'd left school and
taken a job in the supermarket.
Dad was upset at first.
'I wanted you to go to college,' he said.

Now Dad was working again.
He was the manager of a charity shop
Things were looking up at last.
But Jenny didn't fancy the idea of college.
She'd got used to working.
She liked the other girls at the store.
And she'd met Ian.
He'd asked her to marry him.

2

Trish

On Monday morning Jenny sat at her till.
She checked the change in the drawer and
that the till roll was in place.
Another week began.
Looking down the line of girls, she could see
her friend Usha. She waved to her.
They could chat at break time.

Trish Baxter came out of the office.
She went to open the doors of the store.
Trish Baxter was the new supervisor.

None of the girls liked her.

'She was bad enough before,' Mandy said.

'Being made supervisor's gone to her head.
Ian Ross had better watch out, too.
She's trying to get her claws in him.'

This was no surprise to Jenny.
She'd seen the way Trish looked at Ian.
But she said nothing. Not many of the girls
knew she was going out with Ian.
He was very professional at work.
He treated Jenny just like all the other girls.

'Watch out,' she said to Mandy.
'Here she comes.'
Trish came up to them.
'Is everything all right, girls?' she asked.
'Yes thank you,' Jenny said.
'Fine,' Mandy said. 'Ace. Just perfect.'

'There's no need to go over the top,'
Trish said.
She ran her fingers along Mandy's check-out.
'Give this a wipe,' she said. 'It looks grubby.'

'Yes ma'am, no ma'am, three bags full ma'am,'
Mandy said as soon as Trish moved away.
Jenny had to laugh. Mandy was good fun.
She was a big jolly woman.
'Be careful,' Jenny said.
'Don't push Trish too far.'

The store was very quiet on Mondays.
There were never many customers on that day.
It was boring doing nothing.

Jenny was glad when break-time came.
She got her coffee and went to join Usha.
'Hi, had a good weekend?' she asked.
'Not bad,' Usha said. 'More wedding plans.'
'Not more?' Jenny said.
'I thought it was all fixed.'
'So did I,' Usha said, 'but I'm only the bride.
We wanted a quiet do.
Now our mothers have got together.
It's more like a royal wedding.'

'What about you and Ian?' Usha asked.
Usha was one of the few people
who knew Jenny was going out with Ian.
She told Usha all about their row.
'Oh dear,' Usha said. 'Fancy passing up
a dance at the golf club. It's very posh.'
'I know,' Jenny said. 'But it's not my scene.
Most of the members are middle-aged.
I don't know if Ian's speaking to me.'

But she was wrong. On her way back
to the shop floor, Ian stopped her.

'Okay for tonight?' he asked.

He spoke as though nothing had happened.

'I'll pick you up at seven.

We could go for a meal.'

'Yes, fine,' Jenny said.

She was glad they had made it up.

Just then, Trish came out of the stock-room.

'That was a great band on Saturday,' she said.

'I did enjoy the golf club dance.'

'Yes, it was good,' Ian said. 'Will you

excuse me. I can hear the phone ringing.'

He went in to his office.

'Back to work, Jenny,' Trish said.

'Don't hang about. Your break's over.'

She looked at her watch as she said it.

Later that evening, Jenny asked Ian

if he'd taken Trish to the golf club dance.

Ian shook his head.

'No, of course not. What gave you that idea?

She was there with her brother.

I had one dance with her – to be polite.

You're not jealous are you?'
'Well she is very pretty,' Jenny said.
'You've nothing to worry about,' Ian said.
'Trish is just someone I work with.
And she's not my type.'

Jenny leaned back against the seat of the car.
It had been a good evening.
They'd had a lovely meal, a nice drive.
Now they were parked in front of her house.
It felt good with Ian's arm around her.
His kisses still warm on her lips.
'Are you coming in?' she asked.
'Better not. It's getting late,' he said.

Jenny knew her dad didn't mind
her being late when she was out with Ian.
He would be pleased if they got married.
'Have you thought about us getting engaged?'
Ian asked.
'I'd like more time to think about it,'
Jenny said. 'It's a big step.'
'Okay,' Ian said. 'Tell me on Saturday.'

3

Alison's Party

Saturday was the day of Alison's party.
It was for her eighteenth birthday.
The party was to be held in a room
above the King's Head pub.
Alison was Jenny's best friend from school.
When Jenny got there the room was packed.
Lots of her old school friends were there.
She went to give Alison her present.
'Where's Ian?' Alison asked.
'He'll be along later,' Jenny told her.

'Great crowd. And a live band too!
Who are they?' Jenny asked.
'Some friends of Baz's from college.
I'll take you to meet them,' Alison said.

She took Jenny's arm and led her to the stage.
The group were setting up their instruments.
Alison reeled off their names.
'Jenny, meet Pete, Jason, Mick, Tony and ...'
She paused in front of a tall lad
with dark hair.
'Sorry, I don't know your name,' she said.
He looked up from tuning his guitar.

He smiled. It was a shy smile.
'Hi, I'm Phil,' he said. 'Great party.'
He had a nice voice.
'Meet my friend Jenny,' Alison said.
'She's a fantastic singer.'

'What did you tell him that for?'
Jenny hissed.
'Because you're good,' Alison said.
'And I want you to sing at my party.'

It was Baz who pulled Jenny on to the stage.
Baz was Alison's brother.
He was a real clown. Always fooling around.
'Come on girl,' he said to Jenny.
'Let's show them how it's done.
What about a duet?'
Jenny laughed. 'Go on then,' she said.
It would be a bit of fun.

They did one or two old numbers.
Sonny and Cher's "I Got You Babe" and
a couple of songs from the film *Grease*.
Baz was on good form.
Jenny could hardly sing for laughing.
Then he leapt from the stage.

'And now a solo from Miss Jenny Scott,'
he said and handed her the mike.

Jenny spoke to the band.
They knew Celine Dion's latest hit.
She took a deep breath and began to sing.

Afterwards Ian came to claim her.
He pushed his way through the crowd.
'I didn't see you there,' Jenny said.
'When did you get here?'
'Not long ago. I saw you and Baz do
your party piece,' he said.
Suddenly Jenny felt very silly.
It sounded like a put down.

'I need a drink,' Ian said.
'Let's get out of this crush.'
Jenny looked round at her friends.
They were all in casual dress –
tee-shirts and jeans.
Ian was wearing a smart suit and a silk tie.
He looked very handsome but much older
than anyone else there.
Jenny took his arm.
'I'll come with you. Let's get a bite to eat.'

As they were leaving, Alison said,
'Going so soon? Things are just warming up.'
'Sorry, Ian's got to be up early,' Jenny said.
'He's off to London tomorrow.
He's taking over another store for a few weeks.
Thanks for a lovely party. I'll be in touch.'

Jenny went to say a quick goodbye to the band.
Phil smiled his shy smile.
'See you around,' he said.
'Alison was right, by the way.
You have got a fantastic voice.'
Ian tugged at her arm. 'Come on, Jenny.
This noise is getting on my nerves.'

They went downstairs. A taxi was waiting.
'Well,' Ian said. 'Have you
made up your mind?'
Jenny looked at the taxi driver's back.
They couldn't really talk in private.
Ian dropped her off at home.
'I'll call you when I get back,' he said.
'And don't forget. I want my answer then.'

4

The Song

With Trish in charge they had a hard time.
She kept the staff on their toes.
'Do this, fetch that,' Mandy moaned.
'She's a bossy little madam.'
Jenny's mind wasn't really on the job.
She was wondering what to tell Ian
when he got back.
She'd missed him of course.
He was always there to run her around.
To take her out at weekends.

Was that enough? she asked herself.
She liked Ian a lot, but did she really love him?
Did she really want to get married?
She wished he hadn't put this pressure on her.

Jenny watched a young mother trying to do
her shopping with a baby and a toddler.
She knew the girl. It was Anna Thomas.
She'd been in Jenny's class at school.
She looked a mess and her hair was straggly.
At the checkout, the baby began to cry.

'Shush,' Anna said, picking him up.
She began to lay her few goods on the counter.
A tin of beans, some nappies, a cheap loaf.
The little boy at her side picked up
a bag of sweets from the shelf.
Before Anna could stop him, he'd torn it open.
'No,' Anna shouted. She sounded quite upset.
'Mummy hasn't got any money for sweeties.'
She looked at Jenny and said,
'I'm sorry, I'll have to put something back.'
'It's all right,' Jenny said. 'Let him have it.
My treat. I'll put the money in.'

Jenny told Usha about meeting Anna.
'That's one good reason for marrying Ian,'
Usha said.
'He's got a well paid job.
You'd never want for anything.'

Jenny thought about this
as she walked into town.
It was her afternoon off.
She wanted to look round the shops.
Call in to see her Dad.

She found him talking to a blonde woman.
She looked very smart.
She had a brief-case in her hand.
Dad spoke to the woman.
'This is my daughter Jenny,' he said.
'Jenny, meet Mrs Fisher, our area manager.'
'Nice to meet you,' Mrs Fisher said.
'But I'm afraid you'll have to excuse us.
I've just called in to discuss the weekly takings.
I'm in a bit of a rush.'

'That's OK,' Jenny said.
'I'll have a look round the shop.'
She moved to the stand of paperback books.
A tall young man was already there.
He was sorting through the tapes.
It was Phil. He looked up and saw Jenny.
'Hi,' he said, 'I'm glad I ran into you.
I was going to ask Alison for your
phone number. I need a favour.'

'What sort of favour?' Jenny was puzzled.
She didn't know Phil at all.
'Can we talk? Have you got time?' asked Phil.
'It's my afternoon off,' Jenny said.
'We could go for a coffee if you like.'
Jenny picked a quiet table in the café.
'What do you want?' she asked Phil.
'I need your voice,' Phil told her.
'It's exactly right for my song.
Let me explain,' he went on.
'I've written a song for a radio competition.
It needs a strong female voice.'

'Oh no,' Jenny said. 'Not a competition.
I've had my fill of those. Never again.'
'What do you mean?' Phil looked puzzled.
'I once won a talent contest,' Jenny told him.
'An agent said he'd get me lots of bookings.
They were all in really grotty clubs.
I had to stand there in a mini dress
and silver boots, trying to make myself heard.
You couldn't see for the cigarette smoke.
You couldn't hear for the clink of beer glasses.'

Phil roared with laughter.
'Poor Jenny! I can just see it.
You're not really the type to go down well
in working men's clubs!'
'It's not funny!' Jenny said. 'It was awful.'
But soon she was laughing too.
Phil had a way of making her feel at ease.

He took a sheet of paper out of his pocket.
'Take a look. Tell me what you think.'
Jenny read through the words of the song.
They were good, very good.
Phil hummed the melody out loud.
It was beautiful. Just the sort of song
Jenny liked to sing.
A slow ballad, full of feeling.

'Take it home and learn it,' Phil said.
'We'll have to move quickly.
The demo tape has to be sent in soon.'
'How do you know I'll do it?' Jenny asked
'You can't refuse,' Phil said.
'It's perfect for you.'

5

Jenny's Choice

They made the tape a few days later.
Phil had a friend with a studio.
It was in the attic of his house.
The room was full of equipment:
computers, amps, keyboards.
There were wires and plugs everywhere.
Sam, Phil's friend, showed Jenny into
a sound-proof booth.
She put the headphones on.

Her part was done quite quickly.
Then Phil and Sam spent ages working on
the multi-track system.
They added the sound of different instruments.
'First I make a master tape,' Phil told her.
'Then I make a demo tape from that.'

Later they went out to celebrate.
They met up with Alison and Baz for a pizza.
'It's ages since we did this,' Alison said.
'I've missed you Jenny. We haven't seen much
of you since you started going out with Ian.'
'Who's Ian?' Phil asked. 'Not that stuffy
bloke you brought to Alison's party.
I thought he was your boss.'

Jenny felt her face go red.
She hadn't told Phil about Ian.
'He is,' she said, 'but we are going out.
Anyway, Ian's not stuffy.
He's just a serious type of person.'
As she said this it struck her
that maybe that was what was wrong.

She and Ian never laughed over silly things.
She'd had such a good time with Phil
over the past few days.
They were on the same wavelength.
Like now, having fun with Alison and Baz.

At the end of the evening Phil counted out
his share of the bill. It was all in small coins.
'Had to rob the piggy bank,' he said.
'We poor students never have any cash.
I'll have to walk home,' he said to Jenny.
'Still, money isn't everything.'

'Why didn't you tell me about Ian?'
Phil asked. They were standing at her gate.
'I didn't think it mattered,' Jenny lied.
'It's not as if you and I have been on a date.
We've just been working together.'
'What happens if the song does well?'
Phil asked. 'What will you do then?
We'd have to promote it together.'
'I'd discuss it with Ian,' Jenny said.
'He wouldn't want to stand in my way.'

'You don't sound very sure,' Phil said.
'What do you really want Jenny?
You have a great voice.
You could have a career as a singer.
But I get the feeling you're afraid
to risk it. Like the last time –
when you won that talent contest.
You'd give up if things got tough.

Maybe you should stop now. Marry Ian.
Opt for life on a nice housing estate.
Have two cute kids. It's your choice.
Let me know when you've made up your mind.'

With that, he walked away, leaving Jenny
feeling hurt and angry.
She went inside the house.
Her dad was waiting up for her.
'Ian rang, while you were out.
I told him you were out with Alison,' he said.
'I was out with Alison and Baz and Phil.
They're all my friends, OK?'

Her Dad looked upset.
It wasn't like Jenny to snap at him.
'I only did it for the best,' he said.
'You don't want to lose Ian do you?
He's a good man. He's got a steady job.
Not like that lad Phil.
He hasn't got two pennies to his name.'
'Money isn't everything,' Jenny shouted.
'Now if you don't mind, I'm tired.
I'm going to bed. Goodnight.'

6

Good Advice

Ian was back at work on Monday.
He had some important news.
'The firm wants me to take over
the London store,' he told Jenny.
'It's a great chance for me.
I'll go down first. Find us a house.
Then after we're married you can join me.
It'll be wonderful.'
He spoke as if it was all settled.

Jenny didn't get the chance to talk to him.
Ian was too busy in the office.
He wanted to know how Trish had coped
while he was away.
'A move to London, lucky you,' Usha said
when Jenny told her. 'I'd love to live there.
Think of the shops, the shows you could see.'
'I suppose so,' Jenny said. 'It would be fun.'

By the end of the week she still
hadn't told Ian about the competition.
When they were together he always took charge.
He chose the places to meet,
the food they would eat,
and the wine to drink.
Jenny was swept along by him.
He was so excited about the new job,
she didn't like to bring him down to earth.
Besides, she thought, there must be
thousands of songs in the competition.
The chance of Phil's winning was very small.

It was a shock to hear it on the radio.
She was getting ready for work.
Suddenly Phil's song came on air.
Her own voice filled the bedroom.
She turned the sound up.
'That was one of the six songs chosen
by our panel,' the DJ said.
'In a moment I'll tell you how you
can vote for the song of your choice.'

Jenny spent the rest of the day in a daze.
Had she heard it right?
But there was no mistake.
As she walked into the canteen at break time
the song was playing again.

She didn't hear what the other girls said.
Didn't listen to Mandy's tales about her kids,
Usha's chat about her wedding.
All she could hear was their song.

'That's a good song,' Mandy said suddenly.
'I'd vote for it. What do you think, Jenny?'
She had no idea Jenny was the singer.
Jenny hadn't told anyone at work about it.

Ian caught up with her as she was leaving.
'Okay for tonight?' he asked.
It was clear he hadn't heard the radio.
'No,' Jenny said. 'Sorry Ian, not tonight.
I have to go and see Gran. There's something
very important we need to talk about.'

'That's a wonderful song,' Gran said
as soon as Jenny walked in.
'And you sing it so well.
All my friends are going to vote for it.
Have you come to tell me all about it?'
'No Gran,' Jenny said. 'I need your advice.'

'I can't make up your mind for you, Jenny,'
Gran said later.

'Everyone expects me to marry Ian,'
Jenny said.
'And what about Dad? He'd be so upset?'
'You can't marry someone just because
other people expect it. I'm not sure
you really do love Ian,' Gran said.
'I think you were flattered he chose you
from all the other girls.
Oh yes, he's very good looking.
He's got loads of charm.
But what have you got in common?
You seem to have had a lot more fun
with this lad Phil.
And your Dad's a grown man.
From what I hear, he's getting very close
to that Mrs Fisher he works with.'

Jenny was stunned. Gran never left the home
yet she always seemed to know
what was going on.
'It's your life,' Gran went on. 'Your choice.
A husband or a career.'

7

Happy at Last

The train for London was on time.
Jenny sat there waiting.
She looked at her watch.
It was getting late. Where was he?
He was cutting it a bit fine.

Suddenly she saw someone running
along the platform.
He leapt on the train just as the guard
blew his whistle.

Phil made his way down the train.
He threw his rucksack on the seat.
He sat down next to Jenny.
'Phew, that was close. I got held up.
It would never do to miss the prize giving.
Blow our chance of a record contract.'
He took Jenny's hand.
Then he looked into her eyes.
'Are you ready to be a star?' he asked.